"Clara & Her Nutcracker"

Based on E.T.A Hoffmann's "The Nutcracker"
Adapted by: Lisa K. Winkler
Edited by: Lisa K. Winkler
Cover Art: Ryan Durney
Illustrated & Designed by: Ryan Durney

PUBLISHED BY: Lisa K. Winkler

Edition: 01

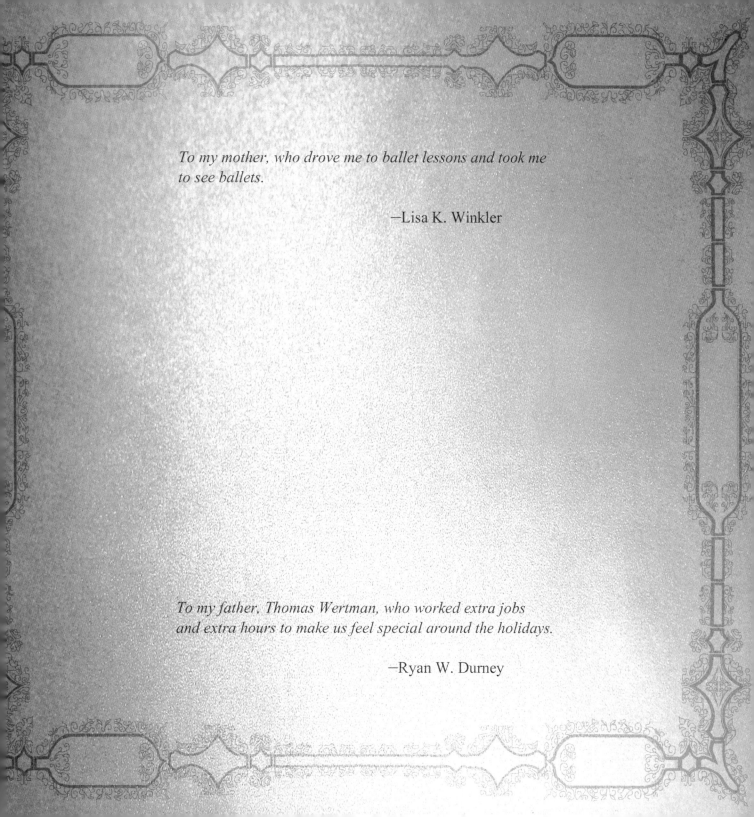

*To my mother, who drove me to ballet lessons and took me
to see ballets.*

—Lisa K. Winkler

*To my father, Thomas Wertman, who worked extra jobs
and extra hours to make us feel special around the holidays.*

—Ryan W. Durney

Clara & Her Nutcracker

written by Lisa K. Winkler

illustrated by Ryan Durney

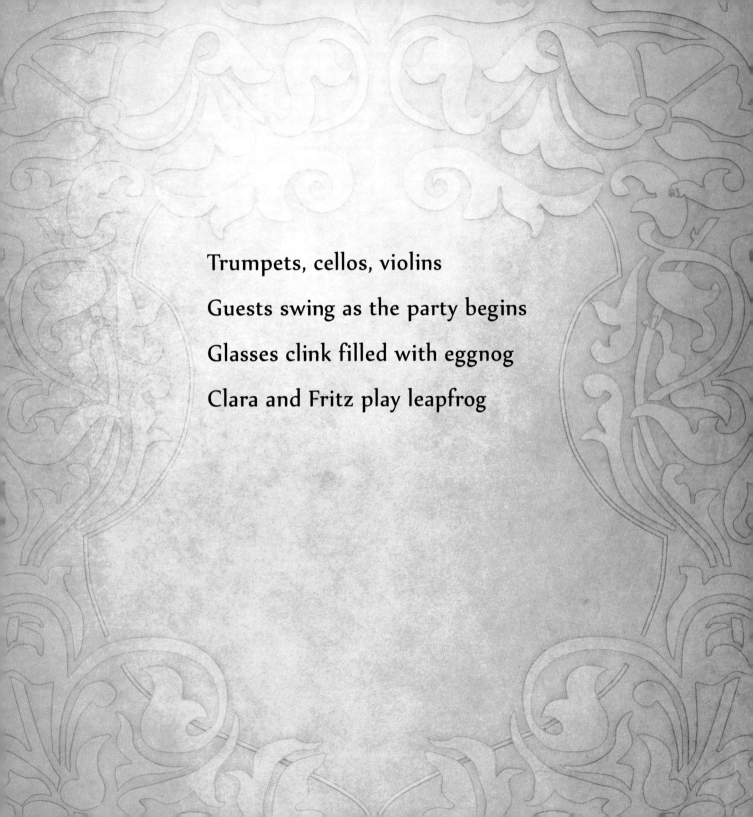

Trumpets, cellos, violins

Guests swing as the party begins

Glasses clink filled with eggnog

Clara and Fritz play leapfrog

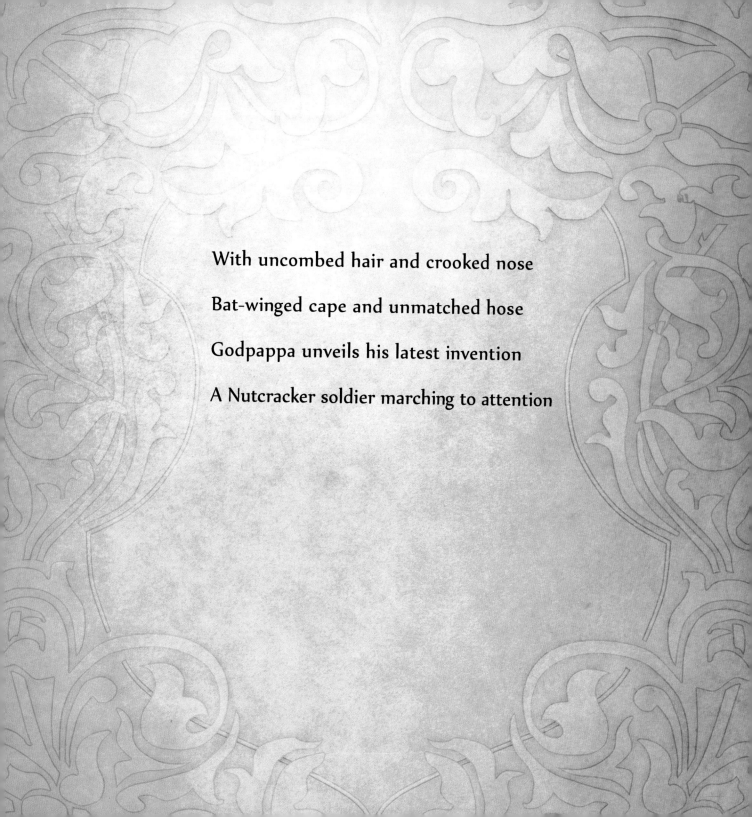

With uncombed hair and crooked nose

Bat-winged cape and unmatched hose

Godpappa unveils his latest invention

A Nutcracker soldier marching to attention

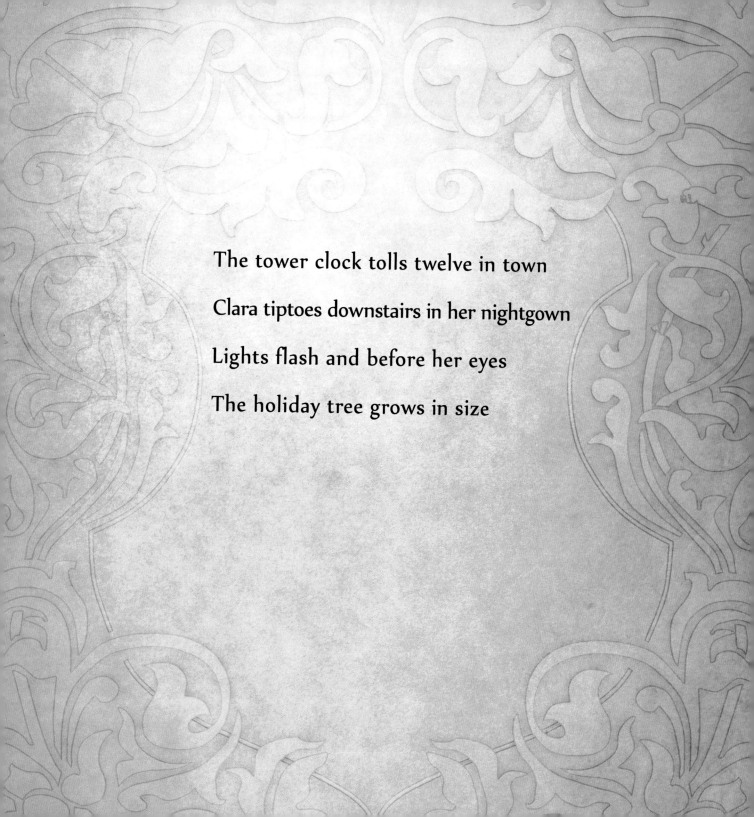

The tower clock tolls twelve in town

Clara tiptoes downstairs in her nightgown

Lights flash and before her eyes

The holiday tree grows in size

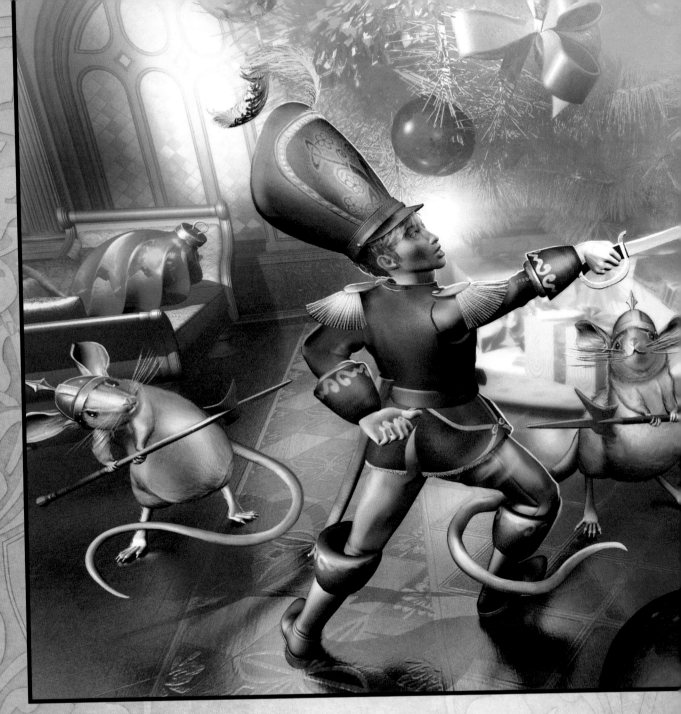

The Nutcracker, no more a toy

Now a teenage soldier boy

An army led by the Mouse King

Surrounds the Nutcracker in a ring

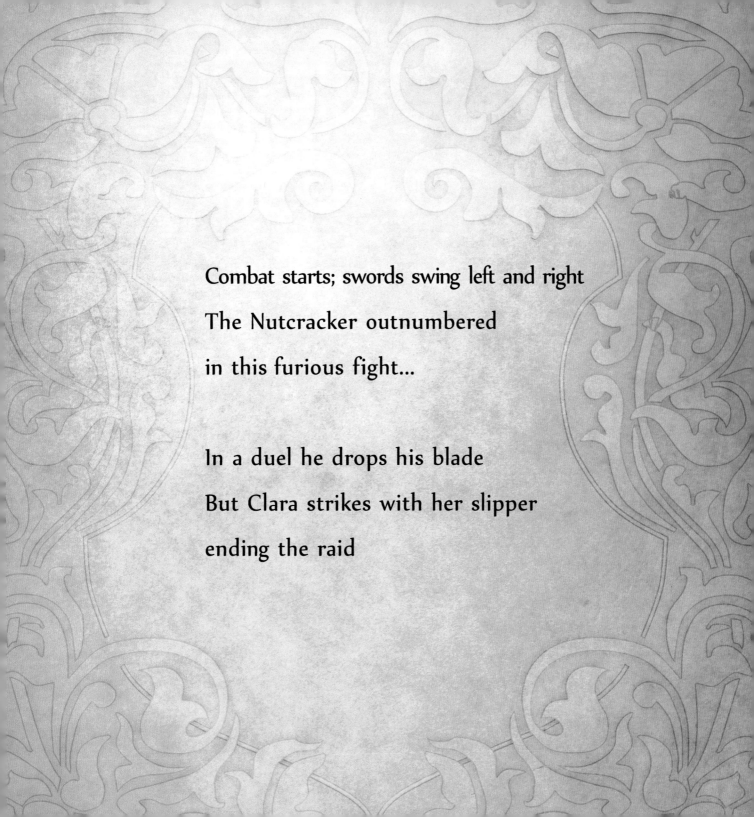

Combat starts; swords swing left and right
The Nutcracker outnumbered
in this furious fight...

In a duel he drops his blade
But Clara strikes with her slipper
ending the raid

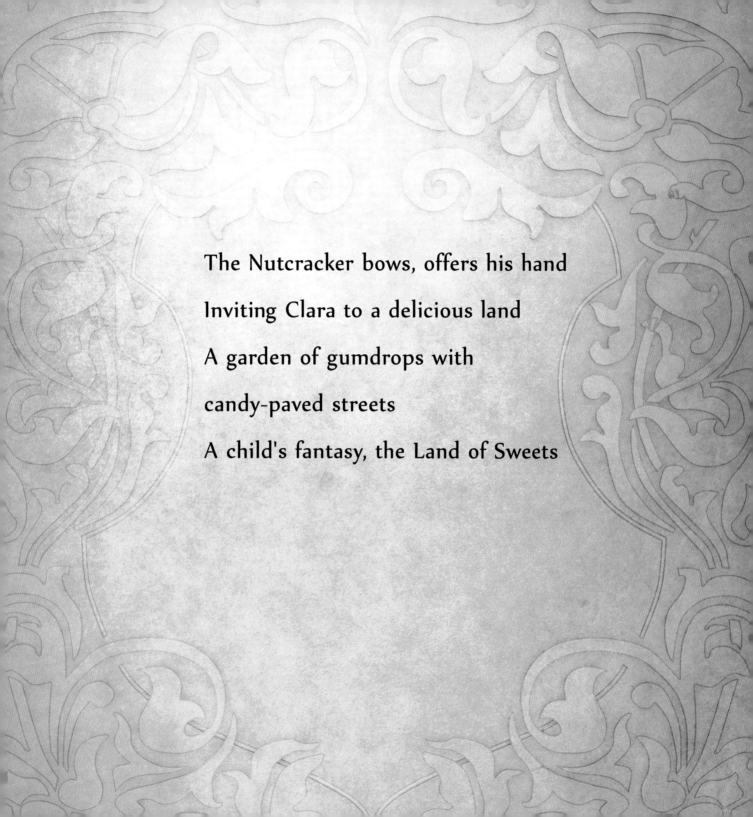

The Nutcracker bows, offers his hand

Inviting Clara to a delicious land

A garden of gumdrops with

candy-paved streets

A child's fantasy, the Land of Sweets

Clash, clang! The Cossacks' cymbals sound

Two dancers leap high then squat to the ground

Legs like sticks stuck straight out

These Russian dancers clap and shout

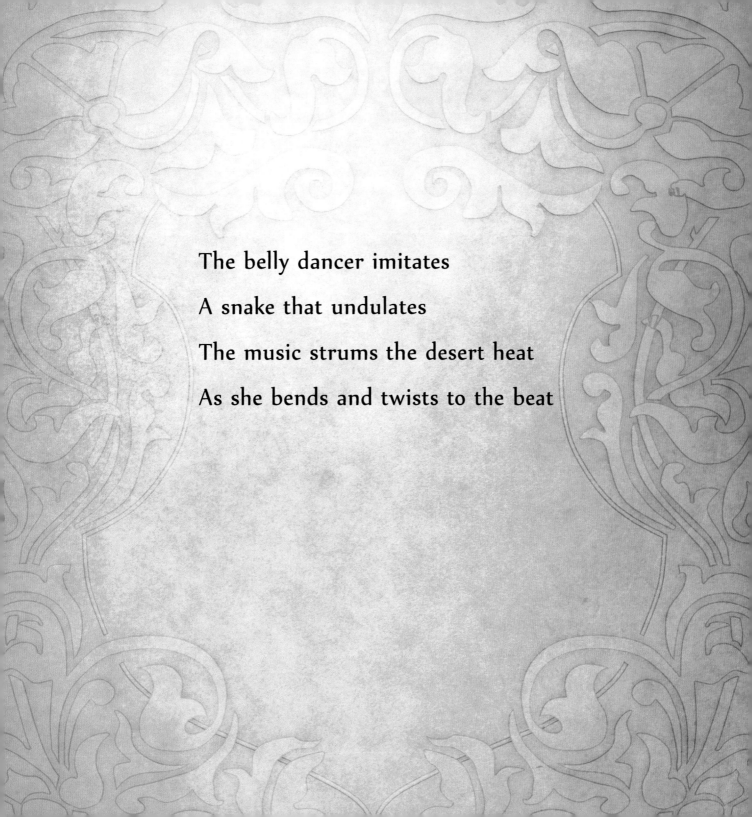

The belly dancer imitates

A snake that undulates

The music strums the desert heat

As she bends and twists to the beat

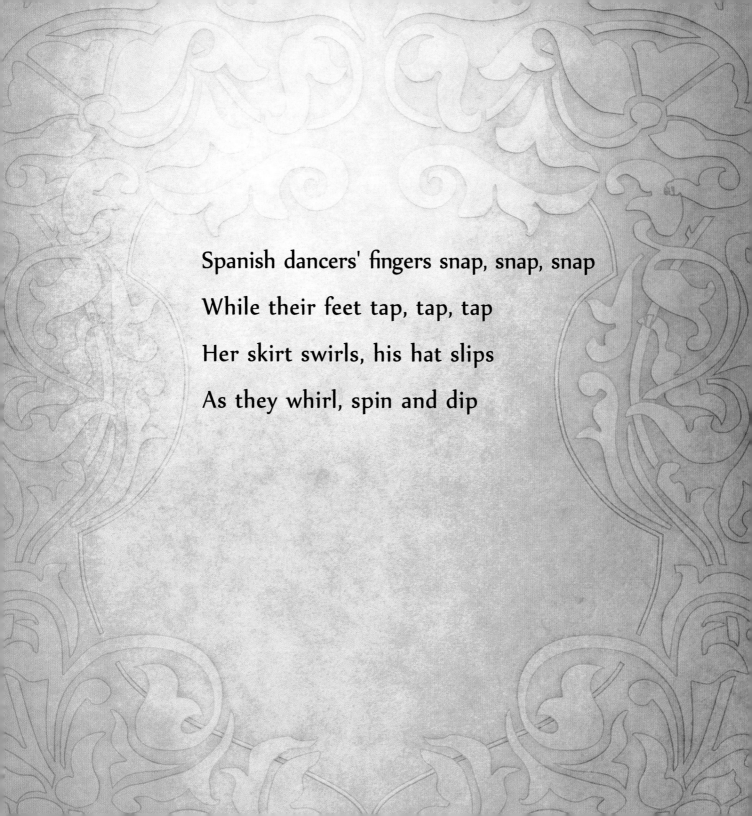

Spanish dancers' fingers snap, snap, snap

While their feet tap, tap, tap

Her skirt swirls, his hat slips

As they whirl, spin and dip

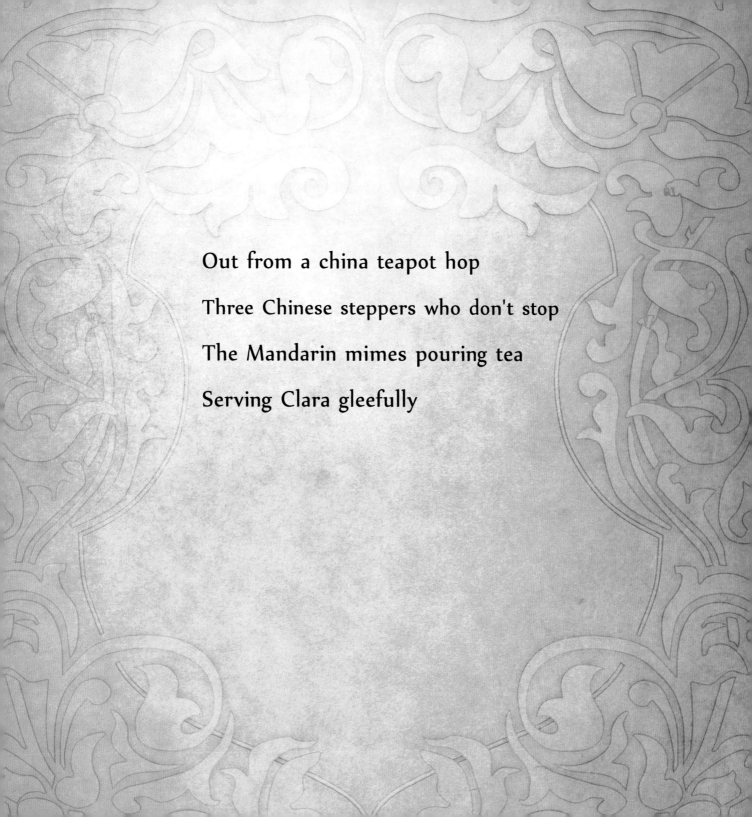

Out from a china teapot hop

Three Chinese steppers who don't stop

The Mandarin mimes pouring tea

Serving Clara gleefully

From Mother Ginger's skirt scamper

Little puppets playing together

Cartwheels, handsprings, jumping jacks

Tumble, jumble until called back

Daisies, poppies, and pansies

Arabesque and sway with ease

Zinnias, daffodils and marigolds

One by one perform a cabriole

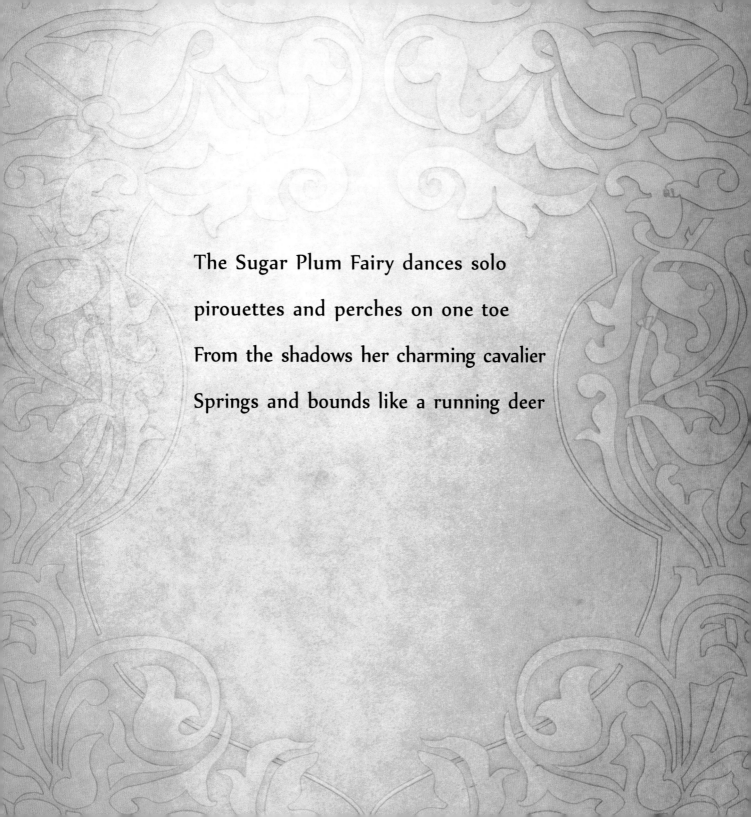

The Sugar Plum Fairy dances solo

pirouettes and perches on one toe

From the shadows her charming cavalier

Springs and bounds like a running deer

Before night turns to day

Clara and Fritz depart by sleigh

The way lit by moonbeam

Or did she only dream?

AUTHOR'S NOTE:

Clara & Her Nutcracker joins a large family of interpretations and adaptations of the original fairy tale by Prussian writer E.T.A. Hoffmann, (1776-1859). The story has been re-told in many picture books and choreographed into many ballets.

Though Hoffmann studied law, he aspired to be a writer. His "Nutcracker and Mouse King," published in 1816, was meant to be a commentary on social class and the restrictive manner in which children were raised to be obedient. In all his writing, he championed the imagination, believing in its power to ignite peoples' dreams and desires.

In 1845, French writer Alexandre Dumas (1802- 1870) adapted the story into "The Tale of the Russian." The Moscow Imperial Theatre commissioned Russian composer Pyotr Ilyich Tchaikovsky (1840-1893) to write the music for a ballet based on the Dumas story and it premiered a week before Christmas in 1892, to great success. It was performed in England in 1934 and then in San Francisco in 1944. By 1954, George Balanchine's staging for the New York City Ballet turned The Nutcracker into a popular holiday ritual.

I've been captivated by the Nutcracker ballet, music and story since childhood. I took ballet lessons until I went to high school. Once or twice a year, my mother would bring my sister Naomi and me to see the New York City Ballet. We saw "The Nutcracker" and many other ballets.

I hope my version of this worldwide tale inspires your imagination like it did mine.

BIOGRAPHY:

Lisa K. Winkler is a writer and educator. She has a Masters in Education with a focus in children's literature.

While she doesn't take ballet lessons anymore, she loves to write, read, knit, cook, cycle, do yoga, and be a grandmother.

www.lisakwinkler.com

Artist's Note:

When Lisa first approached me about a re-telling of the *The Nutcracker,* I admit, woefully, that I only knew the tale from fragmented memories of TV specials over the years featuring the ballet. I love fairy tales and classics like *Alice in Wonderland* and when I did some homework on E.T.A. Hoffman's version, like *Wonderland,* I immediately fell for the high strangeness of the story and was entranced. Also like *Wonderland,* many high-tier artists over the centuries had worked on this tale, and suddenly I felt overwhelmed with the masterful competition of the ages.

Unbeknownst to Lisa, I was obsessed with the idea of a seven-headed Mouse King (that's what Hoffman first wrote!) but I thought it was a little too bizarre for our tone, so I gave him seven golden crowns instead. In my mind, he has done something terrible to seven other rulers of their enchanted realm to steal those crowns!

Lisa, can we please work on a prequel to this story, all about the rise of the Mouse King?!

Also, I remember my sketches were very, very Christmassy, but when Lisa told me that it was more about dance and the stage, it all clicked together in my mind. Then and only then did the famous themes start playing in my head. That music plays when I flip through the final book, so I think we did something right. Do you?

BIOGRAPHY:

Ryan Durney is a full-time illustrator in Austin. He has a BFA in illustration and has garnered several awards, such as a *Children's Choice Award* and recently a *Preferred Choice Award* by Creative Child Magazine for the story book *Princess Willow & the Magic Fairy Brush.*

In his limited free time, he writes short fiction and illustrates it, as he's done in his series *Birds of Lore.*

www.ryandurney.com

OTHER TITLES BY THE AUTHOR:

Tangerine Tango is a collection of writings spanning the entire citrus spectrum, from sour to sweet. Edited by Lisa K. Winkler, who has never been 'a basic beige sort,' these colorful slices of life are sad, nostalgic, and humorous. They're about parents and parenting; childhood; food, faith and farewells; jobs and journeys. Empathize, reminisce, and smile.

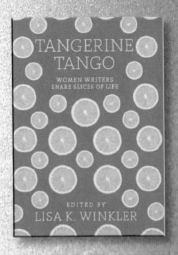

Amanda is so excited to play T-ball. But when the coach announces the batting order, she doesn't get her turn at bat. After three games without playing, she thinks of ways to solve her problem.

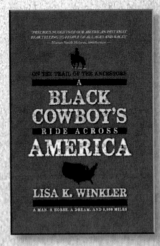

Miles J. Dean, a Newark, NJ schoolteacher, rode his horse from New York to California to celebrate the contributions African Americans made in the settling of the United States. During his six-month, 5,000-mile journey, Dean, a 57-year-old African American, addressed people along the way at schools and colleges, community organizations, and penal institutions.

<u>Other Titles by the Artist:</u>

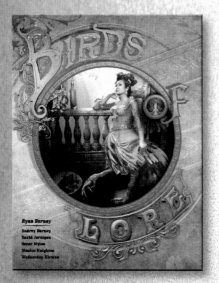

Color Your Dreams is a dream journal, dream interpretation dictionary and Adult Coloring for relaxation, all rolled into one!

Look for several Adult Coloring Books to be released within the year!

Birds of Lore: Follow the exploits of "The Mythologist" as he uses stolen technology to travel time and breach other dimensions in search of creatures that should never have existed. Each entry touches on the origins of a fantasy bird while the wayward Mythologist deals with them in his reality. Based on a mysterious "found journal" and fully illustrated by talented artists, *Birds of Lore* is the closest you can get to mythological bird watching (without losing a finger).

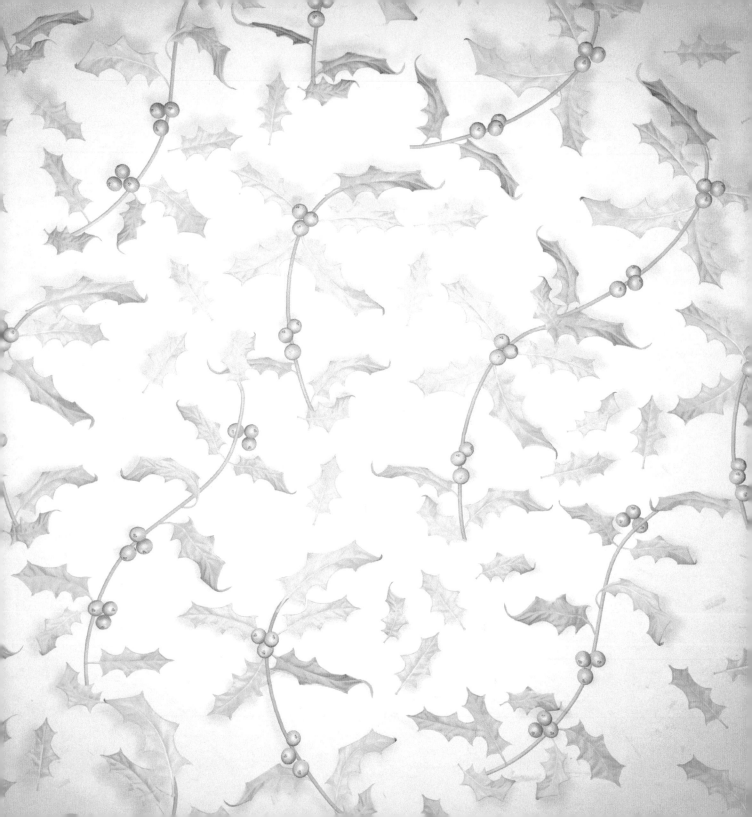